A WOODLAND MYSTERY™

The Hidden Hand

A WOODLAND MYSTERY
By Irene Schultz

The Wright Group®

To Betty and Ted and Granny.   Their long-ago
farm still lives in my heart.

The Hidden Hand
©1996 Wright Group Publishing, Inc.
©1996 Story by Irene Schultz
Cover and illustrations by Taylor Bruce
Map illustration by Alicia Kramer

Woodland Mysteries™
© Wright Group Publishing, Inc.

The Woodland Mysteries were created by the
Wright Group development team.

The Wright Group
19201 120th Avenue NE
Bothell, WA 98011

Printed in the United States of America

10 9 8 7 6 5 4 3

ISBN: 0-7802-7241-2

What family solves mysteries...has adventures all over the world...and loves oatmeal cookies?

It's the Woodlanders!

Sammy Westburg (10 years old)
His sister Kathy Westburg (13)
His brother Bill Westburg (14)
His best friend Dave Briggs (16)
His best grown-up friend Mrs. Tandy
And Mop, their little dog!

The children all lost their parents, but with Mrs. Tandy have made their own family.

Why are they called the Woodlanders? Because they live in a big house in the Bluff Lake woods. On Woodland Street!

Together they find fun, mystery, and adventure. What are they up to now?

Read on!

Meet the Woodlanders!

Sammy Westburg

Sammy is a ten-year-old wonder! He's big for his fifth-grade class, and big-mouthed, too. He has wild hair and makes awful spider faces. Even so, you can't help liking him.

Bill Westburg

Bill, fourteen, is friendly and strong, and only one inch taller than his brother Sammy. He loves Sammy, but pokes him to make him be quiet! He's in junior high.

Kathy Westburg

Kathy, thirteen, is small, shy, and smart. She wants to be a doctor someday! She loves to be with Dave, and her brothers kid her about it. She's in junior high, too.

Dave Briggs

Dave, sixteen, is tall and blond. He can't walk, so he uses a wheelchair and drives a special car. He likes coaching high-school sports, solving mysteries, and reading. And Kathy!

Mrs. Tandy

Sometimes the kids call her Mrs. T. She's Becky Tandy, their tall, thin, caring friend. She's always ready for a new adventure, and for making cookies!

Mop

Mop is the family's little tan dog. Sometimes they have to leave him behind with friends. But he'd much rather be running after Sammy.

Table of Contents

Chapter 1:
The Great Donkey Kick-Off

Ten-year-old Sammy Westburg stood next to a very small donkey.

He patted its neck.

The donkey gave him a sideways look.

Its large eyes were shining.

Sammy said, "This old donkey likes me! If I rode him, he would NEVER throw me off. Look how still he's standing.

"And, anyway, he couldn't. I'm almost as heavy as he is."

Sammy's brother Bill, fourteen, was holding the donkey by its rope.

His face broke into a grin.

He said, "Don't count on riding this one, Sammy. No one at the farm has ever been able to do it. This is ONE MEAN DONKEY!

"Alex says he's the wildest bucking animal he's ever seen ... even at a rodeo."

Sammy said, "Big deal! He must have gone to pretty wimpy rodeos."

Kathy, their thirteen-year-old sister, smiled. She said, "The donkey doesn't look that wild to me! No wilder than

Sammy, at least."

Just then Mrs. Tandy walked up. Sixteen-year-old Dave Briggs was right behind her in his wheelchair.

Dave, Sammy, Bill, Kathy, and Mrs. Tandy called themselves the Woodlanders.

They were all visiting Singing Pines Farm.

Alex and Barbara Golden had asked the Woodlanders to come right away. They said it was important.

Sammy said, "Hi, Dave! Hi, Mrs. Tandy! I'm going to get on this donkey ... and STAY on it ... like gum on a shoe!"

He took the reins in his hands.

He said, "Let go of the rope as soon as I'm on him, Bill!"

He swung his leg over the donkey.

He pushed up with his other leg.

He wiggled to get a comfortable seat.

3

Bill let go of the rope.

Sammy sat on the donkey ... for one second.

And then the donkey bucked!

Sammy went flying through the air.

He landed flat on his stomach, and slid forward.

All the breath was knocked out of him.

Dave raced over in his wheelchair. The rest of them ran along with him.

Bill said, "Sammy! Sammy, are you OK? How do you feel?"

Sammy rolled over on his side.

He looked up at Bill and said, "How do you THINK I feel?

"I feel horrible, that's how!

"My stomach hurts.

"My knee hurts.

"And I think my chin is bleeding!"

He pushed himself to his feet and faced Bill.

He said, "My whole life I've wanted to visit a farm. And my first morning here, I get kicked off by a dumb donkey.

"And it's all your fault, Bill!"

"MY fault?" Bill said. "How's that?"

Sammy said, "Because you let go of

the rope when I said to."

Mrs. Tandy laughed and hugged Sammy, even though he was covered with dust.

Sammy pulled free and said, "How much longer until breakfast? I can't wait to hear why the Goldens wanted us to come here!"

Just then they heard a loud, deep-sounding bell.

CLANG ... CLANG ... CLANG.

Bill said, "That's the breakfast bell!"

They hurried into the big farm kitchen.

Linda Garcia, Alex Golden's sister, was just putting some food onto the table.

They had ...

bowls of sliced peaches

bowls of hot cereal

home-made muffins

big pitchers of milk

... and a platter of bacon and eggs.

Sammy counted the place settings.

He said, "Holy cow, Mrs. Garcia! This table is HUGE! There are ten places set. And there's room for ten more!"

Linda said, "First, Sammy, call me Linda.

"And the reason there are so many settings is that there are a lot of us!

"There's my brother Alex and his wife Barbara ... and their daughter Robin. Robin's about your age, Kathy.

"And Granny. And with you five and me, that's ten! And when my husband Ed gets here Friday night, that will make eleven of us.

"At harvest time we have even more hands to feed!"

Sammy said, "Hands? How do you feed hands? Don't you mean mouths?"

Linda smiled. She said, "We old farmers call a helper a HAND."

Sammy said, "Old farmer? You're not so old! And anyway, you're pretty! But you must be tired ... cooking for so many people."

Linda said, "Oh, no, I love it! Ed and I always wanted a big family, but we never had children.

"So we helped Alex and Barbara raise their three daughters. But Robin is the only one who still lives here.

"It's Thursday? Let's see. She will be back from her two-day school trip this morning!"

She added, "Anyway, we were hoping my other brother would settle on the farm and raise a family, too. But Ted was killed in 1972, in the Vietnam War."

Just then Granny Golden and Alex and Barbara came in, and breakfast began.

Sammy wolfed down his eggs. Then he jumped out of his chair.

He got up and grabbed a pen.

He started drawing on his paper napkin. He drew a family tree!

It looked like this:

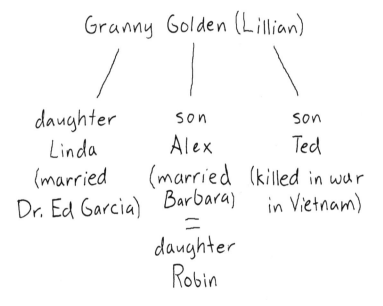

Granny Golden (Lillian)

daughter	son	son
Linda	Alex	Ted
(married	(married	(killed in war
Dr. Ed Garcia)	Barbara)	in Vietnam)
	=	
	daughter	
	Robin	

Sammy said, "I've GOT to get this straight!

"Granny Golden is Linda's and Alex's mom, right?

"And Linda and Alex had another brother named Ted, but he was killed in the Vietnam War, right?"

Bill poked Sammy.

Kathy turned red.

But no one looked mad, so Sammy went right on talking.

"Alex Golden married Barbara, and Robin is their kid, right?

"And Linda married Dr. Ed Garcia, and they bought this farm, right? And you all live here?"

Linda smiled. "Good work, Sammy! You figured it all out."

Alex said, "Everything but the reason why we asked you here.

"We all knew Dave's parents from

before their accident.

"And we wanted to meet you, of course. You're Dave's new family.

"But that's not the only reason we invited you. It's time to fill you in on a mystery!"

Chapter 2:
An Elf at Work?

Alex said, "There are some strange goings-on around here.

"We hoped you Woodlanders could find out who's behind them. We know you're good at solving things."

He grinned. "Or maybe there's no answer. Maybe no one's doing anything. Maybe we are just HAUNTED!"

Granny Golden laughed and said, "Haunted? Hogwash!

"Someone is helping us around here, we just don't know who."

Her snow-white hair was piled on top of her head. Wispy curls circled her face.

She wore a huge blue apron over a black dress. Her skinny little legs stuck out below. Her feet were hidden in fuzzy blue slippers.

She snorted a little. "Haunted! My own son talking about ghosts!

"Barbara, you sweet apple dumpling. You never should have married this clown!"

She picked up a wooden mixing spoon and tapped her son Alex on the head.

He laughed and said, "Well, Mom, then maybe it's an ELF at work!

"Remember the story of the shoemaker? An elf secretly helped HIM at night."

Sammy said, "Oh, I know that one. Then the shoemaker sees him. He makes a pair of shoes, to thank him.

"The elf puts on the shoes. But he dances away, and never comes back."

Alex said, "That's the one! Well, the elf must have danced on over to our farm.

"Barb, read your list of what's happened since last March."

She took a piece of paper out of her pink shirt pocket.

Just then the kitchen door opened. A girl walked in. She smiled at everyone. "Hi!" she said, and hugged her mother.

Barbara said, "This is Robin, everyone, my sweetest and youngest!"

15

Robin wrinkled her nose.

Linda said, "And, Robin, these are the Woodlanders we've been telling you about!"

Sammy said, "Hi! I'm Sammy. And that's Dave, and Kathy, and Bill, and Mrs. Tandy!"

Barbara said, "Honey, you're just in time for breakfast.

"And you're just in time to hear my list of all the work that's been done by our mystery helper."

Robin said, "The hidden hand, AGAIN?

That whole thing gives me the willies. Can I read off the list?"

She put down her backpack. She sat down at the table and started to read.

"Loose boards nailed down tight on barn.

"Shed roofs mended and fences fixed.

"Cows brought into the barn during a storm."

Alex said, "That sure saved some of our new calves. A bad thunderstorm hit, and none of us were here."

Linda said, "At first we each thought the others had done these things. We thought we were just forgetting to tell one another.

"But as time went on, we realized someone else was helping us. Read the rest, Robin."

Robin went on. "Fallen trees sawed into logs.

"Logs split for firewood.

"Dog with broken leg left at our door."

Barbara said, "That's Bush over there!"

She pointed to a fluffy, middle-sized white dog lying near the stove.

She said, "He's cute and sweet, but with the brains of a chicken. And he hates cigarettes!"

Sammy said, "What's so dumb about that? I do, too!"

Linda said, "But when he sees one, he stamps it out. He burns his paws every time. That's not too smart."

Alex said, "But he's a good watchdog. Well, except on the nights he forgets to come home."

Granny waved her wooden spoon at Bush. She said, "Keep that animal out of my SIGHT!"

Barbara said, "Poor Granny. Last week Bush sneaked into her room.

"He saw Granny's nightgown on a chair.

"He loves Granny, and the nightgown smelled like her. So he took it outside and chewed it to bits.

"There were pink scraps all over the barnyard!"

Bush knew they were talking about him. He wagged his tail. It hit the kitchen broom leaning against the wall.

19

The broom fell with a BANG!

Bush jumped straight up into the air.

He raced under the table, on top of everyone's feet. Then he landed flat on Granny's toes.

She said, "Off of me, you big lug!" But Bush didn't move one inch.

So Robin went on reading the list. "Lightning fire put out in woods, hand-woven basket put in barn."

Granny joked, "I think Alex is doing it all. To give us a thrill. He's such a bad boy."

She patted her son on the back.

Alex gave her a hug. Then he said, "The point is, some hidden hand is at work here. A hand we don't know. Can you help us solve the mystery?"

Sammy jumped up. He said, "Sure! What are we waiting for? Don't just sit there eating like a pig, Bill! Let's go!"

Then Sammy stuffed a whole muffin into his own mouth.

Bill laughed and stood up. He patted both of Sammy's stuffed cheeks.

He said, "Come on, Oinker. Swallow that down! Let's start our detective work!"

Chapter 3:
A Bird and a Bush

The Woodlanders went outside.

Robin grabbed a couple of muffins and followed them.

Bush came dancing out.

Suddenly, a white duck appeared from around the back of the house. It hurried over to Bush.

Bush lay down. The duck climbed up onto the dog's paws! It rubbed its bill against Bush's nose.

Robin said, "They're best friends. A bird and a Bush. A perfect match!"

Alex came out to join them. He said, "Say, maybe I'll take you all fishing one day.

"Years ago I put baby fish into our pond. Some of them have grown into real whoppers!"

He held out a tin dish. "See this dough here? Granny saved it for me from bread-making.

"I make it into fish bait. I just mix it with some cheese. Then I let it dry a little."

Sammy said, "Oh, let me mash them

together for you. I love to mash things."

Then everybody rolled the dough into marble-sized balls. They put them onto the tin dish.

Alex covered the dish with plastic. He put it on a fence post. He said, "If I don't put this up here, Bush will eat it. Well, bye for now. I have work to do."

They all waved good-bye.

They started walking toward the pond with Robin.

Bill pushed Dave's wheelchair over the rough spots.

Sammy said, "What do you catch in this pond, Robin?"

Robin said, "Sunfish. Or bass."

Bill said, "Hey, Sammy, maybe there's a giant squid in there. With an eye that's fifteen inches across! I saw a picture of one in my science book."

Sammy said, "That would be too big to live in this pond. Besides, squids need ocean water. You can't scare me."

As they walked along, Kathy said, "Well, I just read about some huge beavers. They lived millions of years ago. Some of them were nearly as big as horses."

Mrs. Tandy laughed. "Maybe a giant beaver's around here somewhere. This farm is huge. No telling what might be living on it!"

Sammy said, "Maybe the hidden hand is a monster BEAVER!"

Robin pointed at the pond. She said, "Look at the monster in the pond right now!"

It was Bush, paddling around with the duck on his head!

They kept going until they came to a hilly field.

The rows of corn had been cut short. They made a yellow pattern against the black earth.

The flat part of the field was plowed in straight rows.

The hill was plowed in circles all around to the top.

Robin said, "See that? That's contour plowing."

Sammy said, "CON-toor? What's contour mean?"

Dave said, "Shape. Contour plowing follows the shape of the land. Good farmers don't plow a hill up and down.

27

Rain could wash the dirt right off it. Just clay would be left."

Robin said, "Dave's right!"

Sammy said, "I bet you didn't know all that, Bill!"

Bill said, "Sure I did, Sammy. We studied contour plowing in school last year."

Sammy ran around behind Bill.

He bumped his knees into the back of Bill's knees.

He wrestled him to the ground.

Then he ran away, up the hill.

He yelled, "Can't catch me, Mr. Know-it-all!"

He reached the top.

He looked toward the woods in the distance.

They saw him lean forward for a better look.

Then they saw him turn and run back down.

His hair was as wild as a haystack.

He was shouting as he ran toward them.

And he looked scared!

Chapter 4:
Was It a Body?

Bill ran to meet Sammy.

He yelled, "What's wrong, Sammy!"

Sammy shouted, "You aren't going to believe this!   There's a BODY lying on the other side of the hill ... down near the woods! A man's body!"

Bill said, "A body? Are you sure it's a body?"

Sammy said, "Well, he's not moving! He's just lying there on his back! What should we do?"

Dave said, "Quick, Sammy! You and Bill run to the house and get the others. I'll wait here."

Robin said, "I'll go with them."

Kathy said, "Mrs. Tandy and I will wait with you, Dave."

Bill, Sammy, and Robin ran off to the farmhouse. In a few minutes they came running back.

Robin's parents and Linda were with them.

They ran up the hill with Sammy so they could see the body.

Sammy pointed down to where he had seen it.

All they saw were some old fallen trees that had turned white from the sun and rain.

Alex said, "I don't see a body, Sammy. Could you have mistaken an old tree trunk for a body? You know, old trees do take on awful funny shapes."

Sammy said, "No way! I saw a man's body lying out there.

"It was face up.

"Right there next to the woods. This side of that little path.

"It was a man dressed in army jungle clothes."

Bill said, "If Sammy says he saw something, he saw it."

Alex said, "Well, I'll tell you what it probably was. You see, Singing Pines Farm used to be two farms.

"That path ran between them.

"At one end of the path is the road.

33

At the other end is the best little fishing stream you ever saw.

"I bet someone parked on the road ... then headed for the stream on foot. Maybe he decided to take a nap in the sun."

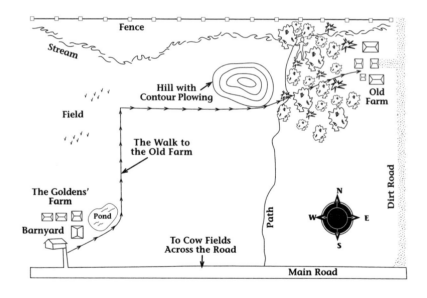

Linda said, "That's probably it. It is such a warm, perfect day for the end of October.

"Well ... I hate to go back. But I'd better get to the house and finish my work."

They walked back down the hill to where Dave was waiting with Mrs. Tandy.

Dave said, "No body?"

Alex said, "Nope. Not that we could see, at least."

Barbara said, "Why don't we all take a little walk before we go back to work?"

Alex said, "Fine. We should while we can ... a cold wave's moving in. By tonight it's supposed to drop to forty, and rain.

"And by tomorrow we are supposed to get an inch of SNOW!"

They walked along for a while, looking at the beautiful fall colors.

35

Finally Linda said, "Well, here's the start of the woods. We should be on our way home."

Alex said, "If the rest of you go east through the woods here, you'll find something interesting. Robin will show you."

Sammy said, "More interesting than a BODY?"

Alex smiled. "You decide. It's a hundred-year-old farm.

"No telling what shape the buildings are in, though. I don't go there all that much. Too busy keeping up our own place.

"And Robin's only been there with me along. We don't like her to go there alone."

Robin said, "I love the old farm! There's an old rotting barn. And an old farmhouse, with an outside trap door to a root cellar. And—"

Sammy broke in. "A ROOT cellar? Is it made of roots?"

Barbara laughed. "It's a deep hole dug in the ground. It's where farmers used to store fruits and vegetables year-round."

Alex said, "A few still do. It keeps them from getting too hot or too cold.

"Apples … carrots … cabbages … beets … potatoes.

"A lot of them are root vegetables. That's how a root cellar got its name."

Mrs. Tandy said, "People used root cellars to hide from tornados, too."

Kathy said, "I remember that from *The Wizard of Oz!*"

Dave said, "What else is on the old farm?"

Linda said, "A chicken house and a tool shed. The buildings have been rotting for years.

"So remember, be careful! We don't want you to get hurt falling through a rotten floor."

Sammy said, "Oh, boy! I'm dying to see it! Come on!"

Alex said, "Just a minute. See that fence over there?

"It's the longer way, but follow that fence. You might get lost trying to go through the woods."

Robin said, "We won't get lost. I know the way."

Sammy said, "And don't worry. I have a compass in my pocket just in case."

Bill said, "But, Sammy, I thought your compass didn't work anymore. Remember, you left it next to a magnet in your drawer?"

Sammy said, "Ha! Look here! I bought a NEW compass!"

He turned the compass until the letter N lay under the pointer. "See? North! Now we can find EAST!"

Kathy said, "Anyway, I'm glad you can come with us, Robin."

Robin said, "Me, too, because I won't be able to go around with you tomorrow. I have school.

"But the rest of today, I'm free!   So let's go!"

Alex, Barbara, and Linda waved good-bye and turned back toward home.

And the Woodlanders and Robin set out to find the old farm.

Chapter 5:
The Scary Old Farm

They started through the woods.

Sammy said, "Hey, wait up!

"A little worm is taking a free ride on my shoelace!

"I have to stop and get him off. I don't want to step on him."

They all stopped.

He lifted the worm off. Then he dashed in front of the others.

He shouted, "Ha ha, slowpokes! I'm going to find the old farm first! Too bad for you, Bill!"

He ran into the thick woods.

And he DID get to the old farm buildings before the others.

He took one look.

Then he turned right around and dashed back.

He grabbed Bill's hand tight, and didn't let go.

He said, "I changed my mind, Bill. I'll stick with you."

They walked out of the woods together.

They took a long look at the old buildings.

Bill said, "Holy cow!   This looks like the set for a horror movie!"

Kathy peeked into the broken-down barn.   She said, "Look, you can see the sky through part of the roof."

Bill pushed open the toolshed door. He walked in.

Dave looked in and called out, "Let me take a look at those rusty tools on the workbench, Bill."

Bill handed some out to him.

Dave said, "Hey! It's a hand-made screwdriver ... and hand-made scissors ... and some pliers.

"I bet they're as old as the farm is.

"But, boy, is this strange!"

Kathy said "What, Dave?"

Dave said, "These old scissors are rusty. But look! They have really shiny edges. Someone must have sharpened them."

Sammy said, "Maybe old tools just stay sharp better than new ones."

Bill put the tools back and said, "Right, Sammy. Come on, let's look around."

They pulled Dave up onto the sagging

front porch of the house.

They all went inside.

There was only one piece of furniture inside, a log bench.

Mrs. Tandy sat on it. She said, "Say, this is in great shape for being a hundred years old.

"Why, look, someone's nailed the old joints to make them strong!"

The kitchen was dark.

They tip-toed in.

A tin dipper and a cracked pitcher hung on the wall.

Fastened to the edge of the sink was a funny metal post, with a handle and a spout.

Kathy said, "That's an old kitchen pump!"

Robin said, "It must have rusted up years ago."

Sammy lifted the handle and looked

up into the spout.

He said, "I wish it still worked."

Then he pumped the handle up and down.

SPLASH!

Water gushed out ... straight into his face.

He snorted like a pig.

Bill couldn't help laughing.

Sammy said, "Stop that, Bill. I got water in my nose. If I drowned you wouldn't laugh!"

He pumped out more water and splashed it on Bill.

Dave said, "Why would this pump still work? Alex says no one has taken care of this old farm for years."

Sammy said, "That's right! Do you think the hidden hand is working around the OLD farm, too?"

Dave said, "Well, if he is, it's going to take a long time to find him!

"There are all these old buildings to search. And there must be fifty acres of woods.

"And an acre is nearly five thousand square yards!"

Robin said, "Dave, how do you know all this stuff?"

Sammy said, "Because he's a living dictionary, that's why! And if he isn't careful, his skin's going to turn into printed paper!"

Dave said, "At least then I'd always have something to read!"

Bill said, "Come on. It's eleven o'clock already. Lunch is at noon. We only have one more hour to look around."

Sammy said, "Bill, I'll search the hay loft with you and Robin."

Dave said, "Kathy, how about if you and I search the main floor of the barn?"

Kathy turned bright red.

Sammy said, "Boy, Kathy, you look like a beet! You should go find that root cellar and store yourself in it!"

Then he ran off a little way and started singing,

"DAVE and KATHY
SITTING in a TREE
K-I-S-S-I-N-G!
FIRST comes LOVE ..."

Mrs. Tandy called, "Stop teasing your sister, you old pest! Now, let's see.

I think I'll look for that root cellar myself."

Fifteen minutes later they had searched the barn's main floor, the hay loft, and the old chicken house.

Suddenly they heard a loud cry.

"OUCH! HELP!"

It was Mrs. Tandy!

Chapter 6:
The Big Hole

They found Mrs. Tandy.

She was sitting on a thick layer of straw outside of the old farmhouse.

Her left knee was bent up to her

chin.   Her other leg was out of sight, below her.

She looked like a one-legged grass-hopper!

Kathy cried out, "Mrs. Tandy, what happened? Are you OK?"

Mrs. Tandy called, "Come over here, kids, and pull me out!

"My leg is down in a hole! I'm stuck!

"And by the way, I think I found that root cellar!"

They ran over and lifted her up. Her leg came back through the old rotten trap door.

She sat back down on the ground.

Kathy hugged her.

She felt both of Mrs. Tandy's legs. She said, "Nothing feels broken. See if you can stand up on your own."

Mrs. Tandy got up, but she groaned a little.

Sammy said, "Your leg will probably be really sore tomorrow!"

Mrs. Tandy said, "Tomorrow! I ALREADY feel like I have a twisted knot for a knee!

"But at least I found the cellar. Now who'd have thought to look for a trap door under all this straw?"

Dave said, "What's that straw doing here, anyway?"

They brushed it aside.

They lifted up the trap door.

53

The sunlight poured into a big, deep hole ... a small room, dug deep into the hard-packed earth.

They looked in and saw a wooden ladder.

Bill and Sammy climbed down into the cellar.

Robin called, "What do you see down there?"

Bill called, "Nothing! Just a big circle of wood! I think it's a huge barrel top! It's leaning against a wall!"

Sammy said, "Oh, yeah ... and an old plastic bowl!"

Mrs. Tandy said, "Well, if that doesn't beat all. All that straw covering, and nothing down there!"

Bill and Sammy climbed back up.

Bill said, "I wonder why the root-cellar floor isn't muddy. I thought it would be a mess."

Robin said, "Me, too. That old trap door must have a million holes the rain could get through."

Sammy said, "Uh-huh. And it must be pretty rotten, or you wouldn't have fallen through, Mrs. Tandy. You're tall and stringy, but you're pretty light."

Mrs. Tandy said, "Thanks a lot, Sammy ... I think."

Kathy said, "Well, look at this!"

When she put the door back down, she saw what she hadn't noticed before.

A sheet of plastic covered the trap door.

Dave said, "No wonder the floor was dry, Robin. Your dad probably used this cellar years ago. He must have water-proofed it.

"We better get a big leaf bag from Linda. We should fix up the hole Mrs. Tandy made."

Sammy said, "What a drag! All we've found so far is a barrel top and an empty bowl."

Dave said, "But don't forget the pump ... and those tools ... and that log bench."

Robin said, "I hate to change the subject, but we should go. It's already nearly lunchtime."

Sammy said, "Rotten rats! We were just getting started! Well, I'm not leaving now. I'll come back to the house later."

Bill winked at Robin. He said, "I'm not leaving Sammy alone. So you'll all have to go back and eat without us.

"Please explain to Linda why we had to miss the fried chicken ... and mashed potatoes ... and gravy ... and fresh-baked bread.

"And eat an extra piece of that home-made apple pie and ice cream for us!"

Sammy said, "Wait a minute! Is THAT what they're making?

"I guess I'll go eat, after all. I don't want to disappoint them. I guess we could come back here later."

So they all went back to the farm house.

Mrs. Tandy stopped near the fence post where Alex put the fish bait.

She said, "The sky's really clouding up. Maybe we should take in these dough balls in case it rains."

She took the plate down.

But the dough balls were gone!

Robin said, "Hmm ... Dad must've taken them inside already."

When they walked into the kitchen, Linda asked, "Did you see anything exciting at the old farm?"

Bill said, "Nothing much. We sure didn't find your mysterious helper.

"But we did get into that nice, dry root cellar. Did you know the door's been water-proofed with plastic?"

Kathy said, "And the old kitchen pump works great! Sammy here can tell you ALL about it."

Sammy made his poison-spider face.

Mrs. Tandy said, "And I liked that log bench in the living room. We thought maybe the mystery man fixed it up."

Linda said, "Well, I'll be!

"That must be my brother's work!

"He used to say he'd fix up the old farmhouse when he found some spare time.

"Then he and Barbara could have a place of their own. I bet he's trying to surprise her!"

Dave said, "Lucky they aren't in for lunch yet. We would have ruined his surprise!"

Sammy said, "Well, we'd better eat pretty fast ... because after lunch I'm going to crack this mystery, once and for all!"

Chapter 7:
The Chicken House

It started to rain during lunch.

It tapped on the tin roof above the kitchen fan.

Sammy said, "This rain better stop.

And it better not ruin our hunt!"

But the rain kept on, not heavy, but steady.

Alex said, "This looks like it could go on for quite a while.

"It's a good time for Barbara and me to drive into town to shop."

Sammy said, "Rats! Now there's nothing to do!"

Robin laughed. "Nothing to do!" she said. "There's never NOTHING to do on a farm!"

Linda said, "You're welcome to join me for the next couple of hours. I'm going to clean out the chicken house!"

Sammy said, "You mean the place where the baby chicks run around? SWELL!"

Robin said, "No, she means the place where all the big mama chickens live. SMELL!"

Sammy said, "Well, a little smell doesn't scare me. Let's go."

They hurried through the rain to the chicken house.

All the walls were lined with boxes. In every box sat a chicken.

Sammy said, "Good grief! SMELL is right! I bet there are a million chickens in here!"

Linda said, "More like a hundred and fifty. Here we go! First we put some feed outside. It doesn't hurt the chickens a bit to eat in the warm rain."

Robin called, "Here, chick, chick, chick!" She threw some dry corn outside.

Most of the chickens rushed out the door.

Linda said, "The next thing we do is wet down the old straw in the nesting boxes. That will make it stick together.

"Wet straw is easier to pull out of the nests."

Sammy said, "Let me do it, OK?"

Linda set the hose to a fine mist.

She handed it to Sammy.

He sprayed the straw in the first ten nests.

But at the eleventh nest he came to a dead stop.

Two beady little black eyes looked out at him.

He said, "Just a minute! What about THIS nest? A hen's still in it! How do I spray it?"

Robin said, "Just reach in under her and lift her out."

Sammy said, "Not on your life! She looks CRAZY! This is a killer hen! She will bite me to pieces!"

Kathy said, "Don't worry, Sammy. Chickens don't bite."

Dave said, "Birds don't even have teeth."

Sammy said, "They don't NEED teeth. A girl at school got bitten by a bird ... the school parrot! It bit her with its beak!

"The girl was wearing gloves. But she should have worn earmuffs. The parrot walked right up her arm and bit her on the EAR!

"I'm not going to let a killer chicken do that to me!"

Robin laughed. She reached under the chicken and said, "See, like this. She might peck at you a little, but she moves right off."

The chicken jumped out of the nesting box ... and ran out the door.

Bill said, "So what's next?"

Linda said, "Take out the old nest straw. Drop it onto the floor.

"Bill, here's a pitchfork. Why don't you pitch the straw out into that wheelbarrow?"

Then they put new straw into each nesting box.

Sammy said, "Sheesh! Where's the mystery helper when you need him!"

Bill and Kathy dumped the wheelbarrow onto a pile of dirt.

Linda said, "Rotten straw and chicken droppings make really rich dirt. It grows wonderful vegetables."

Sammy said, "YUCK! I'd never eat vegetables grown in THIS!"

Linda said, "Too bad. You already did at lunch."

Sammy said, "That's disGUSTing!"

They took a last look at their job.

Linda said, "Good work! Well, it's still raining. Want to go see the baby chicks come out of their shells?"

They all did.

As they came up to the shed, they heard, "Cheep. Cheep. Cheep."

There, running around on the floor, were about a hundred fluffy baby chicks. They were bright yellow, and no bigger than tennis balls.

Sammy pointed to some eggs that were in a white box, covered by a round, see-through lid.

He said, "Hey, what IS that? An oven for baking eggs?"

67

Mrs. Tandy laughed. She said, "You're almost right, Sammy. But it isn't a place to bake them. Only to keep them warm."

Sammy said, "Wait a minute! That egg just shook a little!"

Dave said, "That's a chicken trying to break free! This thing is an incubator, Sammy." He said the word like this: INK-you-bait-er.

Kathy said, "It's a place to hatch eggs into baby chickens."

Linda said, "Right. But some of our hens lay eggs that we eat or sell. They lay their eggs in that hen house.

"Barbara takes the eggs out of the nests every morning.

"If she's going to sell the eggs, she puts them into the cooler.

"And if she's going to cook with them, she puts them into the kitchen refrigerator."

Sammy said, "That's a rip-off!

"Those poor hens, losing their eggs!

"I hate that! I'm never going to eat an egg again!"

Bill said, "Sure you won't. Not until the next time you're served one!"

Sammy socked him in the arm.

Just then they heard a noise outside the shed.

It was Barbara!

She said, "Alex and I just got back

from town. Anybody here want to help me until dinner? I'm going to clear out the goat shed!"

Dave said, "Sure, we all will."

Linda said, "Me, too! I've cleaned out sheds for so long, it's a part of me ... like breathing.

"Last month was my first rest from it in years. Dr. Garcia and I flew to a meeting in New York. I didn't clean out the chicken house. Barbara did."

Barbara said, "What? I didn't do it!"

Linda said, "You don't mean it!"

Sammy said, "Wow! Maybe the mystery helper did it. You should add that to your list of things he did."

Dave said, "That's weird that no one saw him do it. He must have worked here at LEAST a couple of hours ... and so close to your house!"

Robin said, "It's a little scary. It's

almost like he's living right around us. But we never see him."

Sammy said, "Don't worry! Super-Sammy is here!"

With that, he spread his arms wide and jumped off the chicken-shed steps ... right into some mud!

It was deep and thick and soft and sticky.

He sank in above his ankles.

When they pulled him out, his shoes were gone.

Chapter 8:
A Cat Explosion

Bill grabbed the pitchfork.

He poked around in the mud.

He felt Sammy's shoes and dug them out.

He hosed them off carefully.

Finally he said, "Now they're OK, Sammy." He sniffed them. "In fact, they're better than ever ... if you're talking about the smell!"

Sammy grinned. "That's true. After P.E. last week, they smelled really terrible!

"Willie Bird held his nose and pretended to faint.

"Everyone laughed at me.

"So I told them the shoes weren't mine ... that I borrowed them from you, Bill."

Bill said, "Thanks a lot!"

He went with Sammy back to the farmhouse. Sammy changed into some dry clothes.

Bill didn't say a word about Sammy's tumble in the mud. He just stared up at the ceiling and grinned.

Sammy socked him on the arm anyway.

Then they dashed back out to the goat shed.

Bush ran with them, bouncing and barking.

A wire fence circled the shed.

Its wires were only eight inches apart.

But Bush stuck his head and front paws through an opening. Then he began to wiggle.

Mrs. Tandy said, "Why, the poor thing! He's going to get stuck! He can't possibly wiggle through!"

But Bush kept on wiggling and wiggling. Pop! His body went through to the other side.

Sammy said, "Did you see that? He looks so big! But under all that fur he must be about the size of a cat!"

Kathy grinned and said, "Speaking of cats, LOOK!"

A stream of cats was flowing out of the goat shed!

Big cats and little ones.

Smooth cats and fluffy ones.

Old cats and young ones.

There were yellow cats and gray ones, black cats and orange ones, brown cats and white ones, spotted cats and striped ones!

They jumped at each other.

They rolled down the steps.

They bit each other's ears.

They raced after their own tails.

Sammy clapped his hands. He yelled, "It's a cat explosion!

"I bet there are twenty of them!

"Look at that fluffy gray and white one! I love him. His face is just like a bulldog's."

Robin said, "His name is Push Nose.

"That one with the long skinny white tail with the yellow tip ... see how she carries it straight up in the air? That's Candle."

Linda said, "The brown one with the big eyes, see him? With wild fur that sticks out? That's Dragon."

Bill said, "You call him Dragon? From the look of his hair, I thought he'd be named Sammy."

Robin laughed. "These cats live in the

77

goat shed. But they chase mice and rats in all the farm buildings."

Kathy said, "Is that why you have so many of them?"

Barbara nodded. "Yep. We lose a lot of corn and wheat to rats and mice and birds. They steal it right out of the corn crib. Right out of the barn.

"So even our cats are workers. They're guards ... good ones, too!"

Dave said, "That's great! If they can't

scare an enemy away, they EAT him!"

The cats danced after them as they all went into the goat shed.

Inside Sammy took one deep breath.

He grabbed his nose and said, "P-U! I thought the chicken house was bad. It was NOTHING next to this!"

Barbara said, "Then you can see why we are cleaning it!"

She took some pairs of rubber boots from a shelf. They all put them on.

The goats walked over to them. Ducks quacked along at their feet.

Just then a goat pushed his nose into Sammy's hand. He licked the salt off. Then he lifted his neck to be scratched.

Sammy said, "I love these goats! Look how friendly they are!"

Barbara said, "Robin loves them, too. Once when she was little she got hold of my lipstick.

"After a while she called me out to the goat shed. She wanted me to see her work of art.

"She had given our white billy goat HUGE RED LIPS!"

Robin said, "Oh, Mom. You always tell that story!"

Kathy laughed and said, "Let's get a goat for Bluff Lake! It could live in our clubhouse!"

Sammy held his nose and said, "Sure, and you could clean out the clubhouse ... without me!"

Linda smiled. She said, "Let's get to work or we will never finish."

She shooed out all the goats and cats and ducks.

Then they shoveled out the shed floor. They hosed it clean. By the time they were done it was 5:00.

And it had stopped raining.

CLANG! CLANG! CLANG!

Robin said, "That's Granny ringing the bell. She's making supper tonight. Let's go!"

They hosed off their boots.

They went into the house.

Sammy stopped inside the kitchen door. He said, "Holy catfish! Is this a holiday or something?"

Chapter 9:
Noodles and Mice, Cows and Corn!

Big platters of food covered the kitchen table.

Candles burned brightly all around the room.

The whole kitchen was trimmed with skinny white streamers ... hanging over every cupboard door ... over the towel racks ... even over the backs of all the chairs.

Dave said, "What are all the streamers for?"

Granny said, "Those aren't streamers. Those are home-made noodles!

"I made them this afternoon. They're hanging up to dry.

"Come, sit and eat. But don't lean back on my noodles!"

After supper, between bites of pie, Linda said, "Alex, I think we have another job to add to the list of what the mystery helper has done.

"It's the chicken house. I thought Barbara cleaned it last month. And she thought I did. But she didn't. And I didn't!"

84

Alex said, "So our hidden hand was at work again, was he? We really need to track him down."

He looked at his watch. "I see it's time for evening milking.

"Who wants to chase the cows in for me? They're right across the road."

The Woodlanders all wanted to.

Alex said, "Just walk up behind the cows and shout.

"They'll head for a tunnel that goes under the road. They'll come straight to Dave and me in the barn.

"Robin, why don't you go with them and show them how?"

So Mrs. Tandy, Bill, Kathy, Sammy, and Robin crossed over to the field.

They walked up close to the cows.

Sammy said, "My gosh! Look how big they are close up!

"I'm not going to shout at those cows.

I don't shout at animals as big as pick-up trucks!"

Robin laughed. She said, "They won't hurt you."

Mrs. Tandy said, "It's OK, Sammy. You don't have to. Kathy and I will yell!"

Sammy said, "I can do it. I'm not really afraid. I'm just kidding."

But he moved behind Bill. He held on to Bill's arm. Then he shouted, "Hey, you cows! Get going, or my big brother will get you!"

The cows didn't even look at them. They just walked through the tunnel, straight into the barn.

Dave and Alex were waiting for them.

Alex let Bill wash the big, full udder of the first cow. Then he attached the milking machine to it.

He let Sammy start milking another cow by hand.

Sammy sat on a three-legged stool.

He saw four finger-like things hanging from the udder.

He said, "Hey, what are these?"

Alex said, "They're called teats. Take hold of two teats, really tight. That's right, one teat in each hand. Then pull down on each one, in turns."

87

Sammy said, "What if she doesn't like me doing that?"

But in a minute milk sprayed into the pail.

Dave said, "Doesn't milk have to be heated to kill the germs in it?"

Alex nodded. "Usually. But these cows have been tested. Their milk is safe to drink as it is."

Robin said, "Here, Dave! Try a sip! It's still warm from the cow!"

She dipped a cup into the pail. They all tried a taste.

Kathy said, "It's so thick and creamy, it's almost as good as dessert!"

When they finished, Bill said, "That was fun. What else can we do to help?"

Alex said, "Well, you know how corn is covered with husks? I have some special corn ... next year's seed corn for planting.

"I have to strip off the husks and take the corn off the cobs.

"Want to help with that?"

Mrs. Tandy said, "Sure! You mean now?"

Alex said, "Well, yes, if you're not too tired. How about you, Robin? You must be beat. You slept on the bus last night."

Robin said, "No problem, Dad. I like husking."

Alex pointed to a closed door in the corner of the barn.

He said, "The seed corn is in a pile on the floor in that room.

"When the job's done, we can take it into the house. We store it there in the basement ... safe from field mice!

"Bush goes downstairs all the time ... and he's a pretty good mouser, for a dog."

Mrs. Tandy said, "When I was little, I thought I was a pretty good mouser myself. Once I cornered a field mouse in a corn crib.

"I picked him up by the tip of his tail."

Sammy said, "Wow! Did you get to keep him?"

Mrs. Tandy said, "KEEP him! He

walked right up his tail and bit me. I let him go, FAST.

"I was too scared to tell anyone. Lucky for me I didn't get rabies!"

Sammy said, "I'd sure like to see a mouse."

Alex said, "Maybe you'll see one when I open that door ... but I hope not.

"Just the same, stand next to me."

He opened the door of the storeroom.

Suddenly he yelled, "OH MY GOSH! WILL YOU LOOK AT THAT!"

Chapter 10:
The Thank-You Basket

Everyone ran up to look inside the room.

They saw an old chair.

A hill of corncobs lay to the left of it.

To the right lay a huge pile of corn husks.

And near the door was a pile of full burlap sacks.

Alex opened the one nearest him.

It was loaded with seed corn, already husked ... off the cobs ... in the bags ... ready to be stored in the house.

Alex shook his head. He said, "Someone spent HOURS working on this. I bet it's the hidden hand at work again! I'll NEVER get used to this!

"Well, I guess we better load the sacks into that cart and get them into the house."

After the corn was all in the basement, they went into the kitchen.

Alex said, "Granny, can you believe it? This time our mystery helper got all our corn ready for spring planting!

"Would you please help me put together a meal for him ... fit for a king?

"We can pack it into that beautiful basket we found in the barn."

Granny said, "You bet, son!"

Sammy said, "Boy, I hope he doesn't take the food and dance off, like that elf."

Alex said, "Well, he can do what he likes. We owe him a lot more than a good meal.

"I've been putting money aside to pay him for all his work.

95

"I'd have had a hard summer without his help.

"Ed and I have been talking about him. He thinks the man wants to meet us, but is afraid."

Granny said, "I've got in mind just what to give him ...

cold fried chicken

bread and pie

new-churned butter

my own dill pickles

fresh-picked apples

... and milk.

Then she added, "Oh, I've got some corned beef, too. That'll go great with the dill pickles. And oatmeal cookies! I just took them out of the oven."

Sammy said, "Oatmeal cookies? That's our favorite kind!"

Granny said, "Then here are some cookies for you hard-working helpers, too!"

Granny packed the food into the straw basket.

Barbara tied a big red bow to the handle. It looked like a gift basket from a fancy store.

They all trooped out to the barn. They put the old chair just inside the barn door. They put the basket on top of it.

Kathy said, "I was thinking ... we should leave a note."

Alex said, "By gosh, you're right. We have to make sure he knows the food is for him."

So they trooped back to the house.

Dave said, "Whoever he is, why do you think he has nothing else to do but help around here?"

Everyone had questions about the mysterious farmhand.

Alex said, "I wonder if we will ever get to thank him in person."

Mrs. Tandy said, "I wonder if he has any family."

Robin said, "I wonder where he lives. And how he gets here."

Sammy said, "I want to know where he learned to sneak around like that!"

Alex said, "Why hasn't he asked for a regular job on the farm?"

Kathy said, "I wonder if it is really a HE! Maybe it's a SHE!"

Bill said, "Well, I bet he or SHE is lonely, always hiding out."

Linda said, "I sure will be happy when my husband gets here tomorrow night. Did you know that Ed is a psychiatrist?"

She said the word like this: sigh-KIE-uh-trist.

Kathy said, "Well, I knew Dr. Garcia was SOME kind of doctor. But I didn't know exactly what kind."

Linda nodded. She said, "His job is to help people think about things more clearly. He'd help this mystery man if we could find him."

Dave said, "Well, let's get the note written. I think I know what we should say."

Kathy said, "Say it slowly and I'll write it down. But I don't think we should make it long ... or ask a lot of questions."

When they had finished, Bill read the note out loud:

"Dear Hidden Hand,

"Linda and Dr. Ed Garcia, and Barbara, Granny, Alex and Robin Golden, thank you for all your help. This food is a present for you.

"They want to talk to you in person. They wonder if you would like a regular job on the farm.

"If you are too shy to talk to them, talk to us. We are the Woodlanders ... four kids and Mrs. Tandy. We aren't scary.

"We are very friendly.

"We will be out walking around the farm tomorrow.

"Sincerely, the Woodlanders.

"P.S. Sammy (he's 10) wants me to tell you this: Don't disappear like the shoemaker's elf."

Linda said, "That letter says it all!"

So they all trooped out to the barn again.

They taped the note to the side of the basket.

Kathy said, "I can hardly wait until morning. Do you think the basket will be gone?"

Sammy said, "I'm not going to wait until morning.

"I'm going to get out of bed every few minutes. I can watch the barn from our bedroom window.

"I'm going to see the hidden hand TONIGHT!"

Chapter 11:
Big Foot

It was early Friday morning.

Bill was half-asleep in the half-dark bedroom.

Suddenly he felt his mattress rock from side to side.

He heard Sammy's excited voice say, "Hurry! Get up!"

Half-awake, Bill gasped, "What is it? An earthquake? Wake Dave up!"

Sammy said, "No, it's a Sammy-quake. And Dave's dressed already."

Bill looked up. Sammy was standing above him, looking down ... with one leg on each side of the bed.

He was making the bed rock like a ship in a storm.

He said, "We slept all night without watching for him! We missed the hidden hand! And it's ALL YOUR FAULT!"

He dropped an armload of clothes right on Bill's face. He said, "How come you didn't wake me up in the night?"

Bill said, "Get off of my bed, you hippo! Since when am I your alarm clock?"

Sammy jumped off of Bill's bed and

threw on his own clothes.

But he couldn't find his socks. He said, "Come help me, Bill."

Bill said, "After the way you woke me up? Forget it!"

Then Bill tried to put on a shoe. His foot wouldn't go in. He looked inside it.

He said, "Sammy! Here are your socks. You stuffed them in my shoe just to bug me!"

Laughing, Sammy grabbed his socks and darted into the hall.

He crashed into Robin, on her way to school.

He said, "Oops, sorry!" and ran back into the room.

Dave called, "Put on warm clothes, guys. It's cold out! And it snowed last night, just like Alex said it would!"

Kathy and Mrs. Tandy were just coming downstairs.

They all walked to the barn together.

They found Alex milking the cows. He waved, and pointed to the basket.

The food was gone!

But there was something else in the basket. It was a small, perfect wooden hen ... carved from a piece of pine.

Its feathers were shavings, sticking out from its body. Its little eyes were dabs of shiny black paint.

And it was sitting in a real bird's nest.

Sammy said, "That's great! Where did you get it?"

Alex said, "It was in the basket. Our hidden hand must have left it."

Mrs. Tandy said, "It's a little beauty. It looks just like a real hen."

Sammy said, "Well? Did he answer our letter?"

Alex said, "I didn't find any answer."

Kathy said, "Oh, but Alex, he did answer. This carving is sort of an answer."

Sammy laughed. He said, "OK, Kathy, tell me what it says then! That he's too CHICKEN to come and say hello to us?"

Kathy said, "Very funny. Look, Sammy, he must have spent a lot of time making this.

"Then he GAVE it to Alex and the others. So he's saying he likes them. And thanks."

Bill said, "I see what you mean, Kathy."

Mrs. Tandy said, "I think his gift says something else, too ... that he wants to make friends with us. If he didn't, he wouldn't have left anything."

Dave said, "But what's keeping him from coming and talking to us?"

Sammy said, "Who knows! Come on, WE have to go find HIM! Let's go search the woods right now!"

Dave said, "Just a minute. Alex, I've been thinking.

"Yesterday at the old farm we saw some things had been fixed up.

"Linda said you were probably the one who did it ... to surprise your wife. But are you really the one?"

Alex said, "Me? Goodness no! When the kids were little we thought about moving in there. But not anymore."

Dave said, "Then it WAS the hidden hand! He must have worked on the old farm, too!"

Sammy said, "Maybe he hangs around there till he goes home at night."

Kathy said, "Hey, you don't think there's a chance that he STAYS there ... that he LIVES there somehow?"

Mrs. Tandy said, "I don't see how he could. There's nothing for him to keep warm with, or to cook with."

Dave said, "Just the same, we should take another look ... after we search the woods."

Sammy said, "It's about time! LET'S GO!"

The Woodlanders searched the snowy woods all morning with no luck.

At lunch Dave told Alex, "Our next plan is to search the fields.

"Maybe we can find a tent hidden

away there ... or footprints in the snow
... something.

"After that, back to the old farm for
one last look."

Alex said, "Then how about if I join
you folks there around three o'clock, after
work?"

Mrs. Tandy said, "Great!"

Later that afternoon the Woodlanders
left the fields.

They went into the woods again, to
get to the old farm.

Sammy stepped on a branch.

It made a really loud SNAP!

Sammy fell, and let out a scream.

Suddenly from behind them came a
crashing sound.

They spun around.

Through the bushes they saw a shad-
owy shape, bent low, running away.
Then the woods swallowed it up.

They ran a little way into the woods.
They saw footprints in the snow.
But not man-sized footprints.
These were HUGE footprints.
The Woodlanders just stood and stared.
At last Sammy whispered what they were all thinking. He hissed, "Big Foot!
"The hidden hand is Big Foot!"

111

Chapter 12:
The Secret of the Cellar

Bill said, "Hold on, Sammy. That was no
Big Foot.

"He may leave big prints, but we all
saw him. That was a man.

113

"Come on, let's follow his tracks in the snow."

The big footprints led out of the woods to the old farmhouse.

The prints went across the porch.

Wet footprints went through the house ... to a corner of the kitchen.

And then they ended!

Sammy said, "Now, how did he disappear like that?"

Dave said, "Hey, look at that big square patch of wood on the floor. Could it be another trap door? To another cellar? One INSIDE the house?"

Bill noticed a finger-sized hole in the patch of wood. He reached in and pulled it up. The whole square of wood lifted out.

Sammy aimed a pocket flashlight into the darkness. He said, "Hey! There's a ladder! And there's stuff down there!"

Dave said, "Don't go down. I have an idea. Help me get outside."

Outside the farmhouse, he wheeled over to the trap door of the root cellar.

Mrs. Tandy said, "Look at that. The door's covered up with straw again."

Dave called loudly, "Please come out. We didn't mean to scare you. We just want to talk to you."

Sammy poked Bill. He whispered, "Dave thinks he's under there, out here! Could he get from the inside cellar to this outside one?"

Bill said, "Maybe. Remember that big barrel lid against the wall? Maybe that covered an opening between the cellars."

They kept watching the straw.

At last it moved.

The root-cellar door lifted up.

The Woodlanders backed away to give him room.

115

Slowly, out climbed a thin, bearded man.

His hair was tied in a long ponytail.

He was dressed in old army jungle clothes.

His feet WERE huge like Big Foot's ... because they were wrapped in rags.

He took a few steps toward them. They noticed he was limping.

He looked at them with sad eyes.

116

Sammy said, "Hi, there! You're the man I saw lying near the path yesterday! I feel terrible that I screamed and scared you today."

The man nodded his head.

He said, "I should have known it was no big deal. But I can't seem to handle sudden noises.

"Yesterday I WAS taking a nap near the path. But then I heard a shout, so I ran into the woods."

Mrs. Tandy stepped toward him. She said, "I'm Becky Tandy. I'm mighty glad we found you."

The man said, "Well, so am I."

Kathy smiled. She said, "We all loved your chicken carving."

The man smiled a little, but he still looked sad. He said, "Well, that was a nice note you all wrote. And that basket ... thank you."

117

Sammy walked up to him.

He touched the man's arm.

He said, "Everyone at the farm wants to get to know you. And I do, too."

Then, without planning to, Sammy reached out and hugged him.

Tears began to run down the man's cheeks.

Mrs. Tandy reached into her pocket and handed him some tissues.

Suddenly a high, thin voice said, "Why are you all standing in the cold like a bunch of silly chickens?"

It was Granny! She had walked over in the snow with Alex and the others.

She said, "Now you, stranger, come back to the farm this minute. There's a perfectly warm house waiting there for you. And fresh-baked bread. And chicken-in-the-pot.

"You look like you could stand a good

meal. You're as thin as a stick!"

Alex said, "So YOU'RE our hidden farmhand! We've been wanting to meet up with you for a long, long time.

"I'm Alex Golden. This is my wife Barbara ... and my sister Linda Garcia. And this is our mother, Lillian Golden ... but everybody calls her Granny."

The man walked slowly toward Granny. He took her hand in his. He said, "I'm Tony. I'm sorry. I'm so sorry.

"I should have come and told you everything years ago." And he started crying again.

Linda said, "Just a minute. You aren't ... Tony Fermi? My brother Ted's Tony Fermi? You ARE! You've come at last ... after all this time!"

The stranger nodded.

The Goldens looked at him in shocked silence.

119

Granny finally spoke. "Well, Tony Fermi, whatever it is you have to tell us, say it tomorrow. I don't want to hear a word of it today.

"First you need a good night's sleep."

In fifteen minutes they were back near the house.

Robin had just come home from school. She was petting Bush.

But Bush saw the others. The dog dashed across the barnyard. He ran toward Tony and jumped straight for his chest.

Robin shouted, "Watch out for Bush!"

Tony caught the dog in mid-air. He held him in his arms while he licked his face all over.

Tony said, "Good dog, good dog. So your name is Bush now."

Bill said, "Then YOU'RE the one who found Bush when he was hurt. YOU brought him here!"

Kathy added, "And on the nights he was missing, he was with you. I bet that plastic bowl in the root cellar is his water bowl!"

They sat Tony down at the table. Robin brought him hot chicken soup. Bill brought him fresh bread, butter, and jam.

Granny cooked up ham and eggs. Linda dished out home-canned peaches.

Later, Alex helped Tony into a hot bath.

He had to half-lift him out after he fell asleep in the tub.

They gave him pajamas and tucked him into bed.

He fell asleep in an instant.

When Dr. Garcia came home that night, Tony was still asleep.

When Linda carried fresh clothes into his room, he was still asleep.

At last they all went to bed ... wondering what this stranger would tell them in the morning.

Chapter 13:
Tony's Story

It was 6:00 on Saturday morning.

Bill looked out of the bedroom, into the hall.

There was Sammy, sneaking into Tony's room.

Bill followed him. He whispered, "Get out of here, Sammy. Let him sleep."

But Tony rolled over toward them.

He said, "I'm awake. Don't go. You remind me of my own boys."

Sammy said, "You mean you have kids somewhere? Then why have you been hanging around here?"

Tony's eyes looked sad again.

Bill changed the subject. He said, "I heard the others in the kitchen. Let's go in together for breakfast."

In a few minutes everyone sat down at the table.

Dr. Garcia said, "Good morning, everybody! Good morning, Tony! I'm so glad to meet you after all these years. I'm Ed Garcia.

"My brother-in-law Ted wrote us so much about you from Vietnam. He really loved you."

124

Sammy whispered to Bill, "Ted is the one who was killed, right?"

Bill nodded yes, and poked him.

Linda was smiling happily. She looked around the table and said, "Now, this is more like it! This is a crowd worth cooking for!"

In front of everybody, she kissed Sammy right on the cheek.

He turned red!

He got mixed-up.

He said, "Robin, peas plass the canpakes."

Everyone, even Tony, laughed.

125

Alex said, "Tony, I can't believe you're here at last.

"We tried to find you for years after my brother died. We finally gave up all hope of meeting you.

"Why did you wait so long to come?"

Tony said, "I was afraid you'd hate me. Because ... it was my fault Ted was killed. I should have been the one who died."

Linda said, "What do you mean?"

Tony said, "In Vietnam, during the war, Ted and I spent our days in a jeep.

"He was the medic.

"I was his driver and helper.

"We dodged snipers' bullets and picked up wounded soldiers. We moved them to the field hospital.

"And every night Ted talked about all of you ... and about Singing Pines Farm.

"I was an orphan with no family. In my heart, you became my family.

"For a year Ted and I worked together. But one day I got sick. I asked him ... I asked him ... "

They could hardly hear him when he finally got the words out. "I asked him to drive. And a sniper got us. Most of the bullets hit on the driver's side."

Dr. Garcia said, "What happened then, Tony?"

Tony said, "I was wounded in the leg ... that's how I got my limp. Anyway, somehow I drove us back. But Ted was dead.

"I was in the hospital for nearly a year and a half after that.

"I met a wonderful nurse there. We got married. We have two sons.

"But I kept having terrible dreams ... about the war, and Ted dying.

"I haven't been able to forget. I feel scared half the time. I can't stand sudden noises. Even city noises scare me.

"Finally one day I knew I had to come here and see you ... to ask you to forgive me. My wife and boys moved in with her folks.

"I took my camping things so the trip wouldn't cost too much."

Dave said, "But when you got here you were scared to face them? So you ended up camping in the cellar all these months."

Tony nodded.

Sammy said, "But what did you eat?"

Tony said, "Sometimes wild plants. Mostly I sneaked eggs and vegetables. I worked my hardest to repay the family.

"Thursday I ran out of food. I ate your bait ... the dough balls you had put out to dry. And then I found that wonderful basket of food. And that nice letter.

"Yesterday I saw the kids again. Somehow I could talk to them … and now to you.

"I only hope you can forgive me someday … for getting Ted killed."

Dr. Garcia said, "Wait a minute, there, Tony. That was a war accident. It wasn't your fault, and no one would ever blame you."

Granny Golden picked up her wooden spoon. She banged it on the table. Every one turned to listen.

She said, "Listen to me, Tony Fermi.

"My son Ted died a long time ago. And that's not your fault. And terrible as it all was, we have gone on without him.

"Now, I'm too old to go beating around the bush—"

Bush thought she was saying his name. He ran to Granny. He dropped a big slimy bone onto her lap.

Granny said, "This dog is not a dog! This dog is a PIG!"

She stood up and dumped the bone on the floor. She kicked it across the room. Bush ran happily to get it. He brought it back to her.

Granny sighed and went on. "Now, the way it seems to me, we have the perfect chance here.

"Linda's been wanting a bigger family for years.

"And Alex has been needing a farmhand. Tony, you're the one for the job! Your limp doesn't seem to hurt your work one bit."

Bill said, "And you hate the city and love the farm."

Kathy said, "And you need a good home for your wife and kids."

Robin said, "And I would LOVE to have some other kids around here!"

Sammy said, "And I bet your kids would love it here, if you keep them off that rotten donkey!"

Barbara said, "And Ed can help you understand that what happened with Ted wasn't your fault."

Linda said, "You can help us, Tony, and we can help you. Let's at least try it and find out if it works."

Granny said, "Now finish your breakfast. Then get on that phone. Fix it up with your family to come here."

She sat down again. She said, "And pass me those pancakes, Sammy. Or as you call them, canpakes."

She laughed her high little laugh. "You think just because I'm old I don't like to eat? This is a party!"

Sammy said, "Then where are the ice cream and cookies?"

Linda jumped up and went to the freezer. She said, "Coming right up!"

She dished out a scoop of peach ice cream onto everyone's pancakes.

Robin brought in the rest of the oatmeal cookies.

Sammy sneaked one under the table to Bush.

Bush grabbed it and lay down near Granny's feet.

Then they all sat there eating and talking ... while Bush dropped cookie crumbs into Granny's slippers.